the blue door

André Brink

the blue door

Harvill *Secker*
LONDON

Published by Harvill Secker 2007

First published in a not-for-sale edition by Umuzi, the South African
imprint of Random House, on the occasion of its official launch
in March 2006

2 4 6 8 10 9 7 5 3 1

First published in Great Britain in 2007 by
HARVILL SECKER
Random House, 20 Vauxhall Bridge Road
London SW1V 2SA

www.randomhouse.co.uk

Addresses for companies within The Random House Group Limited can be
found at: www.randomhouse.co.uk/offices.htm

The Random House Group Limited Reg. No. 954009

A CIP catalogue record for this book is available from the British Library

ISBN 9781846551239

The Random House Group Limited makes every effort to ensure that the
papers used in its books are made from trees that have been legally sourced
from well-managed and credibly certified forests. Our paper procurement
policy can be found at: www.randomhouse.co.uk/paper.htm

Printed and bound in Great Britain by
GGP Media GmbH, Pößneck

It must be! . . .

It could also be different

MILAN KUNDERA

one

There was, first, the dream. Which should have alerted me, except that I'm not normally into dreams. But this one I found strangely disquieting, and carried it with me, like a persistent tune in my head, through the whole of that long day. Until the shocking moment in the early dusk. The kind of moment that once turned the life of Kafka's Gregor Samsa upside down. But this was not fiction. It happened. And to me.

Not that the dream had any direct bearing on what happened in the evening. But in some subliminal way, and with hindsight, there did seem to be a connection which I have not been able to figure out. Nor, I must confess, have I tried. I believe that dreams belong to the night in which they're dreamt and should preferably not be allowed to spill into the day. This time it was different.

In the dream I am embarking on a long journey with my family, moving house. My wife Lydia is there, but also three children, three little girls, very blonde, with very blue eyes. This is perturbing. We do not have children, and after nine years of marriage it still hurts, although both of us have become skilled at pretending it doesn't matter; not any more. Lydia gets into the front of the truck with the driver. The girls are already in the back, perched high up on the mountain of furniture like little monkeys. I join them and we drive off very slowly, the load swaying precariously. It is a sweltering day and the children are perspiring profusely, their blonde hair clinging to their cheeks and foreheads. They seem to have difficulty breathing.

Before we have reached the first corner, I realise that we will never make it like this. We need water for the journey for the children to survive. I start hammering with my hands on the cabin of the truck. The driver stops and peers up at me, a surly expression on his thick face which is turning an ominous purple.

'I've got to get water for the kids,' I explain. 'I left three bottles on the kitchen sink.'

'We don't have time,' growls the driver.

'I won't be long,' I insist. 'They won't survive without water in this heat.'

He mutters a reply, mercifully inaudible, and I jump off. 'Just drive on slowly,' I try to placate him. 'I'll soon catch up with you.'

The girls begin to cry, but I give them a reassuring wave as I trot off into the simmering and searing white day.

Only when I arrive at the kitchen door do I realise that I have no keys with me. Glancing round to give another wave to the children, I hurriedly begin to run around the house to find a means of entry. It takes three exhausting rounds before I spot a half-open window. In the distance the truck is beginning to disappear in a cloud of dust.

I manage to climb into the house and collect the bottles of water. They are ice cold against my chest. But now the window through which I have entered is barred, and I lose precious time rushing this way and that through the house. Everything seems locked and bolted. I become aware of rising panic inside me.

Then at last, somehow, in the inexplicable manner of dreams, I am outside again, still clutching the water bottles to my chest. By now the truck is nowhere to be seen. Only a small cloud of dust hangs in the distance.

I start running. In the heat my legs turn to lead. But I persevere. I have to, otherwise my family will be lost: they do not know where we are heading for, I am the only one who knows the address. On and on I run.

From time to time I catch a glimpse of the diminishing truck. On on on. I *have* to. I just *have* to.

In the distance I can hear the thin voices of the children wailing, more and more faintly. Once I believe I can hear Lydia calling: 'David! David, hurry!'

Then that, too, dies away.

In the ferocious glare of the day I redouble my efforts. But in the end I am forced to admit that it is useless. I shall never catch up with the truck. I shall never see Lydia and the children again.

That was where the dream ended.

two

Throughout the day it accompanied me – the vivid remains of the dream, the sense of loss. A sad intimation of mortality. Which was uncalled for, really: I am only forty-four. I am supposed to be in the prime of my life. In the generally accepted view I have a successful career, a happy marriage, good and sustaining relationships with friends. I have taught a generation or two of schoolchildren a basic understanding of language and of history; over weekends and holidays I have been able to indulge my private passion for painting, to the extent of taking part in a few group exhibitions and of renting my own studio, a garden cottage belonging to a ramshackle old house in Green Point, far enough from our large, comfortable flat in Claremont to offer a feeling of escape and privacy.

Over the years, ever since I first ventured to take part in an exhibition, I had been toying with the idea of one day giving up teaching to paint full time; but some kind of innate caution – reinforced, no doubt, by my family's convictions about the need for a married man to have a 'respectable job' – had always held me back. After another surprisingly successful exhibition in Observatory at the end of last year, several friends suggested that the time for the break had, surely, come. This time they were much more insistent than before.

'There are no kids involved, David,' said my friend Rudy, whom I have known since our university years at UCT. 'You have a wife who is an architect and surely earns enough to keep you afloat. You have, as far as I know, no huge debts to settle, no financial obligations to family or friends, no plans to get involved in risky investments, you and Lydia are both disgustingly healthy, you're in the gym three times a week, there are no threatening illnesses in the family: so why the hell don't you take the plunge?'

Why the hell not, indeed?

Still the memory of my father? Could be. A prudent man, a toes-together kind of man, a man of considered and considerable judgement, who'd spent all his life escaping from the memory of the Great Depression that had ruined his family and landed them in the unaccommodating streets of Johannesburg. A man conditioned by counting his pennies, never to take unnecessary risks, never to stand surety for man or beast, never to borrow from anyone, never to purchase anything that could not be paid for in cash. He gave me the biggest hiding of my life when as a boy of nine I slipped out of the house one Wednesday afternoon when I was supposed to study for a maths test, to go to a funfair, where I spent twenty cents of my own pocket money on the Big Wheel. He never discouraged me in my attempts at drawing and painting – in fact, he occasionally put a couple of my pictures up in his functional grey insurance office – as long as I did not lose my perspective to indulge in such amusing but ultimately frivolous pursuits at the expense of earning a proper living through a decent job. And a decent job was not only one that brought in a steady income, but preferably one that was also of some value to fellow Afrikaners.

He would certainly have frowned at the idea of my renting a studio. That would have been regarded not as a harmless dabbling in art but indulgence in a private vice. But of course he did not know about the place. Very few people did. In the beginning I kept it as a secret even from Lydia, and it was only when – as was her custom – she was dealing with the household accounts at the end of one particular month that she came upon the bill for the rental of the studio and confronted me with it. One of the worst fights of our entire married life. I felt singularly outraged by her accusations of trying to set up some lewd lovenest, as if I had suddenly been stripped naked in public. It was like the day, I was thirteen or fourteen, when my mother found under my bed a tin of condensed milk I had taken from the pantry and she took the strap to me. As if the beating in itself was not enough, she insisted that for such a serious offence the punishment had to be inflicted on my bare backside in the presence of my three younger brothers and two older sisters. I shall never forget that day. And now Lydia was reviving it in all its unbearable humiliation.

It was not the stealing of the condensed milk as such, I felt, which was at stake. That in itself might well have been a punishable offence (though not in such an extreme manner). But it was the invasion of my privacy, its public exposure, which I found unforgivable. Throughout my life I have felt this urge to have a space that was entirely my own, that could not be violated or invaded by anyone. Even, I'm afraid, in my married life with Lydia I have constantly lived with the deep need to keep something to myself which I would never share with her. Not that I ever tried or even wished to cheat on her, to be involved in anything unsavoury, be it some secret passion or a dubious financial transaction. But I *needed* a space, whether physical or emotional, that would be mine only, inaccessible to the rest of the world. Perhaps it was simply the consequence of growing up in such a big family, which made privacy something of a luxury. I remember how often I would fall asleep at night clutching my blankets very tightly to my neck, convinced that, as soon as I had dropped off, someone – a brother, a sister, a parent, a stranger – would steal into the room and strip away the blankets to expose me to their rapacious eyes.

So it took a long time before Lydia's discovery of the studio could be resolved. In fact, for several months I stopped going there altogether. It was no longer *mine*. But in due course the need to draw and paint – or simply the need to smell linseed oil and treated canvases and brushes again – became so overwhelming that I had to go back. After that, the pleasure was always somewhat attenuated, as Lydia developed a habit of dropping in on me unannounced whenever she 'happened to be in the neighbourhood' to share a cup of coffee, fruit juice, a biscuit or a piece of chocolate, even a glass of red wine. But the relationship between us was steady and sure enough to bear the strain. And often her visits would expand into long rambling discussions – holidays imminent or recent, friends and acquaintances, other people's children, the rapes and murders and political scandals of the day – and even, occasionally, into unexpected but quite satisfying little bouts of lovemaking on the floor, the unwieldy couch covered in paint-stained, faded green cloth, once on the long table in front of the window where I usually stacked my painting paraphernalia. After such a visit a fair deal of tidying up was invariably required – Lydia has always been a great one for setting things right, and would insist on helping, even if I might have secretly preferred to see to it myself, in my own good time; if ever – leading to spring cleanings that left me feeling abandoned in a place that had suddenly become alien; a castaway on a desert island. And when, eventually, I would scrape together the courage to take up my brushes and start on a clean canvas, each venture would be, as Eliot would have said, a wholly new start and a different kind of failure. It reached the point where I seriously considered finding a new studio altogether, in a different and distant part of the Cape, Noordhoek or Durbanville or wherever, where nobody, and certainly not Lydia, would track me down again. But I could not bear the thought of risking another discovery, another fight with Lydia.

For the moment I held on, even though I had been using the place less and less during that particular autumn. Perhaps it was simply the cold that was beginning to affect me. There was no central heating in the cottage, only a fireplace in the living room where I mostly painted; but I did not like the fuss of cleaning the grate afterwards.

So there was, I think now, a general sense of something running out, running down. Within a foreseeable future I might have had to clear out. I might have had to return to the small storeroom at my school I'd used as a studio before moving to the cottage. Which would have been a way of giving up. A way, I thought melodramatically, of dying before my death. That, certainly, was how it felt on the morning of that day after waking up from the dream.

I had spent most of the day trying to work, and not succeeding. Starting on two or three canvases, then scraping off the paint or simply abandoning them on the floor against the wall. Partly my desultory mood came from knowing that in the late afternoon I would have to pack up anyway. We were having guests for dinner and Lydia was expecting me to come home well in time with the shopping she had meticulously listed in the morning. Knowing in advance that the working day would have to be cut short before things had run their natural course was enough to unsettle me and break my concentration, inhibit my imagination. And there was still the aftermath of the dream.

three

By late afternoon I collected the things I meant to take home with me – my leather jacket, some mail, a small pile of essays I had hoped to mark during the day, a sketch book, three old drawings I wanted to look at overnight in the hope of finding ideas for the next painting, a gilt frame – and placed them on the small rosewood table just inside the front door. From that moment on I remember in acute detail every single thing that happened, every step I took, as if it was all registered by a surveillance camera.

My car was parked higher up, just off High Level Road, but I wanted to walk. It was only a short distance: down the steep side street to Main Road, and left to the small supermarket. I had come this way innumerable times over the past few years since I started using the cottage, yet somehow they all seemed strange today. Not like real buildings, but like cut-outs of a stage set, two-dimensional, flimsy, hardboard. As if there was nothing at all behind the façades. The old Edwardian house with the green gate hanging from one hinge. The pseudo-Jugendstil block of flats with multicoloured washing suspended on the balconies like a scene from Seurat or Monet. The three 'modernised' houses on the right crouching behind high railings topped with electrified wire. The small box-shaped building with windows boarded up and billboards announcing its imminent demolition. A row of garages with uniform drab brown doors. More evidence of renewal in dollied-up façades, imitation Cape Dutch gables and inane Tuscan chimneys as one approached the Main Road. The streets and people appeared more real than the buildings. Two obese black nannies pushing white babies in prams, one navy blue, one maroon. A small gathering of bergies rolling joints and drinking blue-train from bottles inadequately stashed in newsprint. Two youngsters in T-shirts and jeans labouring uphill and stopping every few metres to kiss and caress, the man barefoot (long, broken, black toenails) and with tousled Rastafarian hair, the girl with bare midriff and the imprint of a chocolate hand on her left breast. An old couple waddling downhill, the woman carrying a worse-for-wear bouquet of daisies and rather faded blue delphiniums. Two small girls bobbing uphill, their faces smudged by large cones of pink ice cream. The streets were rather dirty, littered with beer cans, empty takeaway cartons, crumpled balls of wax paper, several lumps of dog shit, a gaggle of gulls around a dead fish.

Then along Main Road, and into the super-market.

A woman with lank, oily hair served me with hands on which the fingers, like bunches of blotched peas, had been bitten to the quick. 'Thanks, lovey,' she said without looking up. I took the two plastic bags and left, feeling even gloomier than before.

Uphill, then left at the green garden gate which needed a coat of paint, and round the back of the house to my garden cottage.

Just as I am about to unlock the blue door it swings open and a slim young woman comes out on the narrow stoep. She has long curly hair and the blackest eyes I have ever seen. She is wearing a white T-shirt and jeans, and her feet are bare.

'David!' she exclaims as she puts her arms around my neck and kisses me with her full, moist lips.

I cannot move. I want to say something but cannot find my voice. All I know is that I have never seen her in my life before.

Behind her two small children, a girl who seems to be about five, a boy surely no older than three, both as dark and black-eyed as their mother, come running to me with shouts of glee.

'Daddy! Daddy!' they squeal, their voices shrill with excitement. The girl's long plaits swing wildly down her back.

four

The interior bears no resemblance to that of the cottage I left less than an hour earlier. The rosewood table inside the front door is still there, but the things I left on it – the leather jacket, the mail, the unmarked essays, the sketchbook, the drawings, the broken gilt frame – are missing; and everything else is unfamiliar. The furniture, the carpets, the curtains, the pictures on the walls, everything. Even the layout of the place, as far as I can make out, has changed. For one thing, it looks much bigger. From the entrance there is a wide passage with doors on either side, leading to rooms I do not recognise. The ceiling looks higher. From the hall I can see through a door into what appears to be a spacious and somewhat untidy lounge. It has a large fireplace with an ornate Victorian mantelpiece which I have never seen before.

Involuntarily I take a step back to look, once again, at the front door from the outside. This is indeed the blue door I painted six years ago when I first moved in. I recognise the small tortoise-shaped scar left by a flake of paint that has come off, and two parallel scratches just below the keyhole.

'What's up?' asks the young woman. She seems both amused and bemused as she scrutinises me. 'You look as if you've lost your way or something.'

I want to say, 'Who are you? What are you doing here?' But I am unable to utter a sound. And by now the two children have caught up with me, each grabbing me by a leg, clamouring to be picked up.

Apologetic and embarrassed, I dump the plastic bags on the floor and bend over to pick them up, one by one, first the girl, then the little boy. They cover my face with wet kisses. Somewhat hurriedly I put them down again.

'Excuse me,' I stammer. 'I – honestly, I—'

'Ah,' says the woman. 'I'm glad you remembered to bring the stuff.' She relieves me of the bags and turns round to go deeper into the house, moving smoothly on her bare feet (there is only the sensual, almost inaudible, sucking sound of her soft soles on the tiles) while the children keep tugging at my legs.

Then I hear her call from inside: 'David! Where are you?'

I try to move past the children, but with each of them clinging to a leg it isn't easy.

On the way to the passage opposite the front door I pass an oval hall table littered with mail. Noticing, in passing, my name, I stop involuntarily to flip through the envelopes. There are three accounts addressed to me. A card with an invitation to an art exhibition, bearing the name of a gallery on the back. A letter with a typed address: *Mr & Mrs D le Roux*. Then a large envelope, A4 size; looks like a catalogue. As I pick it up, yet another letter falls on the floor. I stoop to retrieve it, and immediately recognise the handwriting. It is my youngest brother's; he has the commendable if irritating habit of sending a photocopied letter every week in order to 'keep the family together'. This one is addressed to *David & Sarah le Roux*.

I am still staring at the address when the woman calls again from the back of the house: 'David? Where are you?'

I clear my throat. Still staring at the envelope, yielding to a sudden feeling of recklessness, I call, 'Sarah—?'

'I'm in the kitchen.'

I try to find my way to where the voice has come from.

The kitchen is large and flooded with light. It looks recently renovated, although it already bears signs of the kind of destruction and dilapidation only small children can wreak: some broken tiles, muddy footprints on the floor, a broken red plastic bowl, tatters of newsprint everywhere, fingerpainted artworks clinging precariously to the fridge, cat's litter and a food bowl scattered near the back door.

Sarah, if that is who the stranger is, is unpacking the plastic bags on a homely old kitchen table in the middle of the floor. The children are clamouring to 'see, see', so I deposit them on the table just to make the noise subside. Which is effective inasmuch as it curbs the decibels, but brings what politicians term unintended consequences in its wake when the boy manages to tear open the pack of sugar and spill the contents across table and floor.

'Tommie!' yelps the woman, lunging forward and managing to save the eggs as the carton slides perilously close to the edge.

'David!' she cries again. 'For God's sake, don't just stand there. Help me!'

It takes a while to unpack everything on the table and deposit the protesting children on a cabinet out of reach of the stove.

'Well!' she says at last. A few strands of her dark hair cling alluringly to her forehead, one of them in a delicate S over her small nose. Her black eyes smile. 'At least you remembered everything, which must be something of a first. Except that you added chocolates.' She accusingly holds up the slabs. 'They were not on my list.'

'Guilty as charged,' I admit.

'Chocky, chocky!' screeches the boy. 'Yes, please,' adds the girl, an angelic expression on her face. 'We were very good, Daddy. And you *promised*—'

'After supper,' says their mother gently but firmly. I am struck by the easy way in which she handles both them and the household. I am conscious of her very dark eyes and unruly hair, the slimness of her figure – she appears to be in her late thirties, but with a litheness that would be captivating in someone ten years younger. And – emphatically – her pretty slender feet. The kind of woman, it occurs to me, with whom I might fall in love. If I were free. But there, of course, is the rub. I am not free. Except that in this totally weird, bewildering situation everything suddenly seems to be up for redefinition.

There must be some mistake. And I must get out of here before it becomes an impossible tangle.

'You have to excuse me,' I say precipitately. 'I'm not sure about what is going on here, but I really have to go.'

'Where?' asks Sarah in obvious surprise. 'You've just come home.'

'I – I forgot to lock my car.'

'Can we go with you, Daddeeee?' pleads the girl.

'No, Emily, you stay,' says the mother. 'You can help me make the sauce for the chicken. And when Daddy comes back he can bath you.'

Squeals of delight.

Flustered, I back out of the kitchen and return to the entrance. I take my time to look around. My throat feels constricted. There is something very wrong here. Perhaps there is an easy explanation for the whole mystery, but right now it escapes me.

As I open the front door a blast of cold wind forces me back. Instinctively I reach for the small table where I left my jacket but of course it is no longer there. Annoyed, and leaving the door open, I return to the passage. From close to the kitchen I call out, 'Sarah, where's my leather jacket?'

She appears in the kitchen doorway. 'What are you looking for?'

'My leather jacket.'

There is a frown between her dark eyes. 'Leather jacket?'

'Yes. I left it at the front door when I went out earlier.'

'But you don't have a leather jacket, David,' she says.

'But I—' I shake my head.

She comes to me. 'Are you sure you're all right, darling?'

'Of course I'm all right! It's just that—' I sigh. 'Never mind. I'll try to sort it out.' Although I do not have an idea of how to go about it.

When I look back from the hall, she is still standing at the kitchen door, staring at me with a puzzled, concerned look on her face, the fingers of one hand pushed into tousled black hair. I feel an urge to go to her, to reassure her, perhaps – preposterous thought! – to take her in my arms and comfort her. But how can I do that? This woman is a total stranger to me.

Behind her I see the children, their eager little faces. Tommie is leaning forward as if preparing to stand on his head. Emily holds one small hand with perfect starfish fingers outstretched towards me. They seem frozen in their positions.

I go out into the wind, pulling the blue door shut behind me.

My car is still where I parked it in the early afternoon, in the side street just down from High Level Road. Without thinking, I slide into the driver's seat, close the door and start driving home.

five

The enormous apartment building in Claremont looms ahead in the early dusk. I have never noticed it before, but today I am struck by how much it resembles Brueghel's *Tower of Babel* – although there is nothing dilapidated about this one. It is vast and solid, arrogantly modern, rising layer upon layer, with yawning glass-and-chrome entrances on all four corners. As there are rows of cars queuing up to enter, I find a parking spot outside in a small side street, about a block away.

I hurry to my entrance at the north-west corner and go to the lift. The inside of the building appears gloomier than usual, which may account for the fact that I find myself in a lift I do not know, on the indicator panel of which only even-numbered floors are listed. Curious, I have never seen numbering like this before. But I shrug it off. Instead of going straight up to 13, I take the lift to 12, from where I can easily mount the single flight of stairs. Except that, for some reason, the staircase is not where it used to be in the past: there are stairs going down from here, but none leading up to the higher floors.

After a while I decide, rather peeved, to return to the lifts and go up to 14, from where I may find a way down. But this lift does not go any higher than 12.

There seems to be no alternative but to go down to the ground floor again and find another lift. However, as it turns out, the one I get into has uneven numbers and does not stop at the ground floor but continues all the way to the basement. Swallowing my mounting irritation, I get out to take another lift. But in the basement all the lights appear to have fused and I simply cannot locate anything. I start feeling my way back to the first lift, but in the dark I cannot find my way at all and have to start crawling along the wall hoping to find an issue of some kind.

After what seems to have been at least an hour I discover a gap in the darkness in front of me. A stairwell, it seems. Only, there are no stairs, either up or down. From what I can make out – but what *can* I make out in that Egyptian dark? – this is just a gaping hole. For all I know it may reach down to the bottom of the earth. Meticulously I start palpating the wall again, centimetre by centimetre. Surely, if I continue this way, keeping the wall on my left, it *must* lead somewhere.

I trip over what feels like a big box and nearly fall flat on my face.

'Fuck it!' I mutter under my breath.

For a while I squat down on the floor. There is no cause for me to get excited. There is a rational explanation for everything. This, after all, is a hypermodern building; there must be logic in its construction. No need to lose my cool. No need, above all, to hyper-ventilate, as my body is threatening to do. Breathe deeply, count to ten, try again.

Another hour: this time I remember to check it on the luminous dial of my watch. Then, unexpectedly, I stumble over an object in my way. A big box.

Can it be the same one as before? But if it is, I have completed a circle without passing any openings or recesses at all, and certainly no stairs or lifts.

By now I can really feel panic tightening my throat. My forehead is wet with sweat.

If only I had a cellphone with me. But that is a part of modern technology that has passed me by. (How many times has Lydia made disparaging comments about it!)

Calm down now. Just take it calmly. Count to a hundred.

And then, inexplicably, my feet find a staircase, leading up. How could I have missed it on my two previous rounds? No matter. I'm here now. I shall soon be out and on my way up to Lydia, who will be most amused. She has in recent months been teasing me about ageing much faster than she.

I keep mounting for an interminable time. Surely this is much more than a single storey? I start counting the stairs. After a hundred and fifty I stop. This is bloody ridiculous.

Now what? Go down again? Most decidedly not.

Up and up. Another hundred steps.

And then, suddenly, rounding a corner, there is a glimmer of light ahead. It grows stronger. My breath is coming in unhealthy gasps, burning my throat.

The light keeps on increasing. After stumbling on for another eternity I find myself back on the ground floor, the lobby I know so well. The whole thing must have been a delusion. Perhaps, I reassure myself, I blacked out for a while and missed some vital clues along the way. It may not be a bad idea to have a medical check-up after the weekend. If it is still Sunday afternoon? I look at my watch. It has stopped.

But at least I have the reassurance of the lobby. There is a row of lifts on the right. Four of them.

I enter the first, taking care to keep the door open until I have consulted the instrument panel. 2 – 4 – 6 – 8 – 10 – 12 . . . up to 20.

I'm not going to make the same mistake again.

I move on to the second lift. Uneven numbers this time, but they stop at 9 and then jump to 19.

The third lift reverts to even numbers.

The fourth has a small white handwritten card stuck to it. *Out of Order.* So what will it be?

I can of course take the stairs. But the idea of thirteen flights does not appeal to me. Especially not after my experience in trying to get out of the basement.

Just stay calm now. Think, David. Think. *Cogito ergo sum,* or whatever.

It takes some time before it strikes me that I may, quite simply, have come to the wrong entrance. This may be south-east, not north-west. I have never made this mistake before, but there's always a first time.

Isn't there? *Isn't there?*

I go outside. The early-evening breeze fans my overheated, throbbing face.

I look up. From this angle the building indeed has a totally different aspect from the one I am used to.

Immensely relieved (but still with a shadow of uneasy doubt in a deep corner of my mind), I proceed along the outside wall of the huge complex until I reach the next corner, marked *North-west*, where I step into the brightly lit entrance hall.

Immediately I feel at home. Of course, yes, this is where I should have entered in the first place.

I have wasted an inordinate amount of time. Curiously, my first thought is not of Lydia, who must be frantic with anxiety by now. (I am such a conscientious and punctual husband, so wholly predictable. Apart from that one rash decision, so many years ago, when I turned down the invitation to leave the country with Embeth, I have never done an uncalculated, unpremeditated thing in my life.) The person I am concerned about right now is, instead, the strange young coloured woman Sarah behind the blue door. She must be worried about me. And the children. The lisping Tommie, the solemnly smiling Emily with her long plaits.

I hurry to the far corner. This time I have no hesitation in opening the first lift, the one I always take.

The instrument panel is reassuringly familiar. 1 – 2 – 3 – 4 – 5 – 6 – 7 – 8 – 9 – 10 – 11 – 12 – 13 . . .

I step inside and press 13.

The lift shoots up at what feels like a dizzying speed. I rest my right hand on the side railing to keep my balance. In the dark mirror I see my face like a pale blotch in the half-dark interior. It looks disembodied. To tell the truth, I do not recognise myself at all.

Only after several seconds do I register that there must be something wrong. I seem to be going too far. I check the panel. It has changed since I stepped inside: the sequence of numbers is quite irregular. 3 – 7 – 8 – 11 – 15 – 19 – 20. At 20 the lift comes to a shuddering halt, but the door does not open.

I press GROUND, but nothing happens. When I try 15 the lift comes into motion, but it swooshes right past the requested floor and once again comes to a standstill only at the last stop, the ground floor. The door remains firmly shut.

20? Once more the lift zips to the top, where it remains motionless. Then down: this time it stops at 15 and the door slides open.

Gasping with relief, I quickly step outside to take two flights of stairs down. But although this floor is clearly marked 15, and the next one 14, there appears to be no 13: the floor after that bears a bold number 9.

Somewhat to my surprise – by now I am ready for anything – the rest of the sequence remains normal and in due course I reach the ground level.

Shall I test the second of the four lifts? No harm in trying.

But although there are numerous buttons on the panel inside, not one of them is marked with a number. They are all blank.

I move on to the third lift. In this one every single button sports the number 20.

As in the first entrance lobby, the fourth lift is marked *Out of Order*.

With grim determination I leave the monstrous building and proceed to the third entrance. *South-east*.

Once again I cannot find a single lift marked with the correct numbers.

At the entrance to *South-west* I find a very old man with a bald head and a beard like a crow's nest. He seems extraordinarily interested in my actions, which alarms me sufficiently to take the precaution of asking: 'Excuse me: I have to go up to the thirteenth floor. Could you please tell me how to get there?'

'Take the lift,' he mumbles indistinctly. 'Press the number thirteen button inside.'

I go to the first, but the moment the door opens I hesitate. Once again the instrument panel appears defective: there are no numbers on the buttons, only the letters of the alphabet.

For a moment I hesitate, before I go back to the Ancient Mariner. 'Does it make any difference which lift I take?' I ask him.

'Not to me it doesn't,' he grumbles.

'Should I rather wait?'

'Up to you,' he says, with what sounds like sneer.

'But I must get to thirteen,' I insist.

'Why?'

'Because I live there.'

'Do you now?'

'Look,' I say, making an effort to remain calm, but aware of the tightness in my jaw and of salty perspiration stinging my eyes. 'There is something funny going on here. But all I want is to get home.'

'Who doesn't?' asks old Methuselah.

'For God's sake!' With a tremendous effort I restrain myself. 'Could you – *please!* – tell me what to do to get to thirteen?'

'Just be patient. Wait like all of us.'

'For how long?' I demand.

He shrugs his bony old shoulders. His face has noticeably withered since my arrival. 'I've been waiting here for three hundred years.' A sigh of resignation. 'But of course, you may be lucky.'

With a heavy heart and tired feet I leave the building. Outside I stop to look up at the rows upon rows of windows. I used to be able to find our windows high up without any problem. Tonight I am not sure. Somewhere up there Lydia must be waiting. Or isn't she . . . ?

I have a distressing feeling of having left her in the lurch. Betrayal of a kind I have committed only once before in my life. This time it is different. But does it not come down to the same cowardly abandonment?

How long have I been here? The hands of my watch still stand accusingly on ten to seven. For all I know it may be past midnight. What has happened in the house with the blue door in the meantime? Are the children still waiting for me to bath them or has the mother taken over my chores? Why should the thought suddenly make me feel guilty, as if I have let them down? I have nothing to do with them, have I?

And Sarah?

Why should the thought of her suddenly perturb me? I don't even know her. Although she seems to be perfectly familiar with me. Suppose, in a way I have no hope of fathoming, she really regards me as her husband? I remember the full, moist touch of her lips on mine. Her black eyes. The movement of her body, her tight buttocks as she walked away down the passage. The sucking sound of her bare feet on the tiles. And in spite of myself I feel my weary step quickening as I walk to where I left the car. If it is still there. If it has ever been there. If I myself am here.

The moment the blue door swings open and I step inside, I see them in exactly the same positions and postures they were in when I left: Sarah with the fingers of one hand thrust into her hair, Tommie leaning forward, preparing to stand on his head, little Emily holding one hand outstretched towards me. As if no time at all has elapsed since I closed the door behind me. It is a most unsettling sensation, but I seem to be the only one to find it strange.

'If you bath them,' says Sarah, 'I'll get on with the food. I've already put their pyjamas in the bathroom.'

'Yes,' I say meekly, once again rattled by the total unfamiliarity of the place, the people, the situation. But now that I have been excluded from the flat where I live, I don't seem to have any choice. And in a curious way it is reassuring to be accepted so unquestioningly. Perhaps, I think, the strangeness is not here, but in me. I may have lost my touch momentarily. Soon, who knows, everything may slot into place again. It is better not to let on how bewildered I am.

'Let's see who gets there first,' I propose, and allow them to race past me with piercing shouts of glee before I follow.

In the bathroom, round the corner in a side passage, the bath is waiting, with large, soft, white towels laid out on a stand next to the toilet, and the children are already half undressed by the time I arrive. In a flash they are in the water, their smooth little bodies as slick as baby seals. A few big splashes cover half of the floor in puddles. 'Watch out!' I warn, alarmed.

'Come on in, Daddee,' orders Emily.

'In, in,' urges Tommie.

I take the precaution of closing the door before I start undressing. My fingers are clumsy with embarrassment, but they seem not to notice anything out of the ordinary and in a few moments I slide in. Fortunately the bath is so full of toys of every description that it isn't difficult to cover myself. But anxious to be out again and dressed before their mother puts in an appearance I go through the motions of a perfunctory wash, then do my best to perform a hasty cleansing job on them – which isn't easy, as they wriggle and splash like eels.

Even after I am out and clothed again, they continue to clamour for my attention. Tommie has imaginary cuts and wounds on his knees and toes to show me, and which have to be kissed and patted before he will let me go. And Emily manages to get her long hair wet and insists on having it rubbed and dried before she will return to her games with a yellow duck and a partially dismembered Barbie doll.

It takes a lot of pleading and rash promising to

coax them out of the water again. Tommie is so busy collecting his boats and fishes and cars that it takes all my energy to dry him and stuff him into his bright pyjamas. Without more ado he runs off. Then it is Emily's turn.

'I'm sure you can dry yourself,' I say when I lift her out to deposit her on the only dry patch on the floor.

She shakes her head vehemently. 'No, I can't,' she says. 'You dry me.'

'Then stand still.'

'You must put me on the table.'

With a sigh I pick her up and stand her on the table where the towels were laid out. But after a brief bout of patting and rubbing, she insists on lying down on her back.

'You haven't done my butterfly,' she says, spread-eagled and with an expression of bliss and mocking on her little face.

'I'm sure you're big enough to do it yourself.'

'But you *always* do it.'

And only after the sweet little butterfly has been

lovingly attended to does she consent to being dressed, exuberantly thwarting me at every turn.

After every button has been done up twice and her long black hair thoroughly dried with a new towel, leaving her fragrant and glowing, does she take me by the hand and lead me to their room off the main passage where Tommie is perched on his small blue bed, engrossed in a humming game of cars and trains.

'Now the story,' says Emily as she snuggles into her own small red bed.

'Which story?'

'*You* know. The one of the three little men.'

'Where's the book?'

'It's not in a book, silly,' she laughs. 'It's *your* story.'

For a moment I am stumped. 'Tell you what: tonight *you* tell me the story of the three little men. You and Tommie can take turns to see who knows it best. Okay?'

It takes a while before they accept.

Emily begins: 'Once upon a time there was a long, thin, white house, and in the house there lived three little men. A little red man, and a little blue man, and a little yellow man . . .'

It is a strange sensation, an echo from a very distant past. I grew up with this story, which my father used to tell us; but I haven't heard it for years and am not sure I can remember it properly. But now I want her to go on, and it is as if the story itself is drawing me into its undulations; it is like entering a place I have forgotten and only gradually rediscover as my own.

'The little red man sleeps in a little red bed,' says Emily.

'A little blue bed,' corrects Tommie.

'A red bed.'

'A blue bed.'

'A red bed, stupid!'

'I think they only get mixed up later in the story, Tommie,' I gently intervene.

'A blue bed!' he shouts, sitting up. 'Just like mine.'

'Red.'

'Blue.'

'Let's see what happens if it is red,' I propose.

'No, blue, Daddy.'

At this point Sarah comes in. She looks amused, but tired. 'How far are you?' she asks from the door.

'Tonight it's our turn to tell the story,' Emily says. 'But Tommie keeps changing it because he's stupid.'

'*You're* stupid!'

'Let Tommie try, Emily,' says Sarah. 'Then we see what happens in his story.'

'But it will be all wrong!' the girl argues, red in the face with indignation.

'Stories needn't be the same every time,' says Sarah. 'It's nice if you don't always know what's going to happen next.'

'But I *want* to know what happens next.'

'Why don't we hear how Tommie tells it, then you tell it your way, and then Daddy can tell it the way *he* likes it.' She smiles slyly. 'And then we can have a vote and see which one we like best.'

'What's a vote?' asks Tommie.

'It's a red thing with yellow spots,' says Emily. 'And it gobbles you up if you don't listen properly.'

'Mum-meeeeee!' wails Tommie.

'All right, you tell us about the beds,' Sarah quickly suggests.

Before Emily can interrupt, he reels off with an air of impish arrogance: 'The little red man slept in a little red bed, and the little yellow man slept in a little yellow bed, and the little blue man slept in a little blue bed.'

And from there Emily takes over and the story runs its course, as it slowly comes back to me from childhood, with the little men building a boat and dragging it to the sea, and a dolphin arriving to take them to the other side, where they visit a little orange woman, and a little green woman, and a little purple woman, in a small round black house; and then the dolphin comes to take them home, but in the dark and in their tiredness after the long day, they tumble into the wrong beds and cannot sleep – the little red man in the yellow bed, the yellow one in the blue bed, the blue one in the red bed. Until someone thinks of putting on the light and they discover the mistake, and each little man gets into the right bed, and they all sleep happily until daybreak.

'Good,' says Sarah as she gets up quickly, and tucks both the children in, and kisses them. 'And now you sleep in your own little beds,' she says happily, 'and after supper Daddy and I will go to sleep in our own bed, and then we'll all live happily ever after.'

seven

If only it could be so easy, I think as we leave the sleepy children and go to the dining room. There is a feeling of foreboding in me. How are we going to sort this out? The mere thought of going to bed with this striking young woman makes my spine tingle. But how can I do that? It is not only the thought of betraying Lydia that troubles me, but the idea that – somehow, even without allowing me any choice in the matter – it may mean taking advantage of Sarah. I have done at least one reckless thing in my life by turning my back on Embeth; I am not sure I can commit another terrible mistake by sleeping with Sarah. (Unless it would be an even greater sin *not* to sleep with her.)

The question remains: how could I be 'taking advantage' of her if in her eyes I am her lawful husband, the father of her children? It is not I who is misleading her. I may be the one misled. I may be deluded, for all I know I may be hallucinating, all of this may be happening in a dream. Her two children may be as unreal as the small blonde girls on the back of the truck when I went home to fetch them water.

Sarah has prepared a delectable chicken dish, with lots of garlic, the way I love it, and with a big salad of greens and nuts to accompany it. 'This looks wonderful,' I say. 'You should not have taken so much trouble.'

'I know you had a hard day,' she replies as she sits down. 'I thought you deserved a special effort.'

'Shall I open some wine?'

'Please, I'd love some.'

'Red or white?'

'Why do you ask? You know I never drink white.'

'One never knows. You always find ways to surprise me.'

'*You're* the one with the surprises.' She smiles. 'Like the candles in the bedroom last night.'

I have to make an effort to keep cool. 'I wouldn't have done it if I didn't believe you deserved it.' And I add, as if to test the name on my tongue: 'Sarah.'

'Why do you say it in such a funny way?' she asks.

'What do you mean: "funny"?'

'I don't know. As if you're not used to saying it.'

'I don't think I'll ever get used to it, really.'

'David.'

I look up from where I have begun to remove the lead seal from the wine bottle on the sideboard behind the table. 'What?'

'You're not having an affair, are you?'

'An affair?!' I nearly drop the corkscrew. 'Of course not. Absolutely not. What makes you ask an outrageous thing like that?'

'You're a bit – strange.' She looks me straight in

the eyes. 'Ever since you came home this afternoon. As if you can't really look me in the eyes properly.'

'It's just that I've been battling with my painting today, without getting anywhere.'

'Yesterday you said it was going so well, you'd made the breakthrough you were waiting for.'

'That was yesterday.'

'You always have an answer for everything, don't you?'

'Try the wine,' I say bluntly, offering her one of the glasses I have just poured.

She gives a little sigh, tastes the wine, then smiles. But her eyes retain their shadows: sadness, accusation, disillusionment. No longer as unequivocally youthful as before.

'Please don't look at me like that,' I say.

'Give me your plate,' she says quietly. Adding after a moment, 'I've had a tough day too.'

'How come?'

'The children, mainly.' She hands me my plate, helps herself to a small wing.

'They're so lovely!' I protest.

'I know. And that complicates it all. I love them, David. But they also keep me away from what I really want to do. You of all people should understand that. You had the guts to give up teaching and paint full-time. But I . . .'

I don't even know what kind of work she does, I think. There is a silence as she looks down into her plate. Then looks up again, a swift, jerky movement of her head; the curly black hair swings back from her face. 'Do you remember all the dreams we once had? Is this what we have been waiting for all these years?'

'We haven't been doing so badly, have we? Only a few years ago we couldn't even have got married. We might have ended up in jail. Now we can lead a normal life together.'

'I suppose it all depends on how we define "normal".'

A completely perverse thought suddenly strikes me: if we have a quarrel now and go to bed full of resentment and unresolved rage, I may not have to make love to her. But is that what I want?

Instantaneously something in me rises up in revolt. What am I thinking? How can I contemplate rejecting a chance like this?

(You rejected it once before, a voice inside me jeers.)

And what about Lydia?

'Let us try to be reasonable, Sarah,' I say gently.

'Jesus, that's *so* like you!' she says with a flash of real anger. 'Always so damn reasonable. Perhaps life just isn't *meant* to be reasonable. It's got to be lived, not discussed, not reasoned. When we first met, there was so much that wasn't anything like reasonable. There was love. There was joy. There was madness.'

I turn cold at the memory of words so shockingly similar to these, spoken with just as much passion, but in a different voice. Could it have been only sixteen years ago? A different world, a different life. (*But that was in another country, and besides, the wench is dead.*)

'We have children now,' I venture. 'We have responsibilities. We are older now.'

'But we're not old yet. For heaven's sake, David, you're forty-four. I am thirty-nine. We still have everything to live for.' A long, slightly shuddering sigh. 'Can you understand that?'

I put out my hand across the table. 'Of course I do.'

'And you will help me?'

'I will.'

She takes my hand. 'Promise?'

'Promise.'

How little, I think, it takes. But how can I live up to it? I have just committed myself to a woman I have never set eyes on before today. A very beautiful, very passionate woman whose hand is at this moment holding mine. And who, once I wake up in the morning, I may never see again.

But in the meantime we have this night. Which may turn into a nightmare.

Or not . . .?

'I'm tired,' she says, almost in a whisper. 'I'm going to bed. Will you clear up?'

'Of course.'

She pushes her chair back. 'Don't be long,' she says in a voice of shadows as deep as the night, and bends over to kiss me on the cheek.

I promise, I think emphatically.

eight

She is already in bed when I arrive, lying on her side, reading, her back turned to me, the outline of her body gracefully traced by the sheet, one smooth brown shoulder exposed.

But it is quite an obstacle course before I get there. First there is the bathroom. Automatically I go to the one where I bathed the children, but it is immediately evident that this is meant for kids only, or possibly for guests. Playing blind man's bluff, I have to feel my way along the main passage where the lights have already been turned off, past the bedroom where the children have been tucked up for the night, towards a glimmer halfway to the left. From the passage door I can see another door leading from the bedroom, to my right, opposite the bed. To my great relief it turns out to be the en suite bathroom. But this is by no means the end of my problems. I decide to spend a few minutes under the shower first: although I have already had a bath with the children, that was a rather hurried affair, and furthermore I need time to reflect on my immediate challenges. Which of the two toothbrushes – one blue, one red – am I supposed to use, which towel is mine? And afterwards, should I proceed to the bedroom naked, or with a towel around my waist, or wearing pyjamas? (Which will be where?)

In the end I decide not to aggravate the situation by wondering about what her expectations may be but simply to follow my inclination, doing what comes naturally to me.

So I am naked when I come into the bedroom and furtively slide in behind her back, trying to hide the evidence of my state of anticipation.

She glances over her shoulder and says, 'Oh.' Which may mean anything.

Fortunately there is a pile of books beside the lamp on what I take to be my bedside table, and I grasp the top one to page through. It is Jostein Gaarder's *Sophie's World*. I've been meaning to read it for a long time, but something has always intervened. Perhaps this is as good an opportunity as any of getting through it. But I soon put it down, all too aware of the gentle undulation of the woman's body next to me. The urge to touch her becomes hard to resist. But I am restrained by the uncertainty about what might happen if I do. And there is the pure visual joy of looking at her. For the time being I do not want to do anything except to look, and look, and look. (How I wish I could paint her as she lies there now, at this moment, so close, so real.)

After a while, from the way in which she remains almost motionless, never bothering to turn a page, I realise that she is not reading either. Waiting for me to make the first move?

I move my hand closer to her, still without touching.

There seems to be the merest hint of a stiffening in her body. But it may well be my imagination. And it is of decisive importance that I be sure before I risk an approach. Because if not . . .

'What are you reading?' I ask. But my voice is so strained that I have to clear my throat and repeat the question.

'Haruki Murakami,' she says, turning slightly over on her back and raising the book to let me see it. '*Sputnik Sweetheart.*'

'What's it like?'

'A strange book,' she says without looking at me. 'I don't think it's entirely convincing, but it's very disturbing.' Now she settles squarely on her back and turns her head to look at me. 'In the key episode of the story the young Japanese woman – what's her name?' She flips through a few pages. 'Yes: Miu. She gets stuck at the top of a Ferris wheel at a fair in the middle of the night. And when she looks around, she discovers that she can see into her own apartment in the distance. And there's a man in there, a man who has recently tried to get her into bed. While Miu is looking at him, she sees a woman with him. And the woman is she herself, Miu. It is a moment so shocking that her black hair turns white on the spot.' Her black eyes look directly into mine. 'Can you imagine a thing like that happening? Shifting between dimensions, changing places with herself . . . ?'

'I think it happens every day,' I say with a straight face.

'What do you mean?'

'When one makes love. Don't you think that's a way of changing places with yourself? The world becomes a different place. You are no longer the person you were before.'

'You're still an incorrigible romantic.'

I am not sure if that is meant as criticism, cynicism, or gentle approval.

'Shall we try?' I ask quietly. This time I put out my

hand and fold it over the gentle roundness that moulds the angularity of her bare shoulder.

There is a tense moment. Everything, I realise, hinges on this. Everything. Not just the choice between yes or no, between making love or turning away, but who we are, where we are, what we are, what may become of us.

At least she doesn't make an attempt to turn away. A moment later, with a small sigh, she closes her eyes. I take the book from her and put it aside. Then I kiss her shoulder.

'David,' she says, as if it is not a name but the introduction to something longer and more complicated. Monologue, soliloquy, poem, reminiscence, memoir, prophecy. Or all of it together. But whatever the rest might be, it is left unspoken.

I push myself up on an elbow and pull the sheet from her. She is wearing a very thin cotton nightdress, full-length, but rucked up to her thighs. I bend over, down, to kiss her knees. She utters a small sound and raises her hips so that I can pull the nightdress up to bare her pubic mound. It is very small and dense, smooth as a sable paintbrush; I touch it with the tip of my tongue.

I speak her name as she has spoken mine. But I have no idea of what it means. 'Sarah.' I do not even recognise my voice.

And so we move through the undulations of our lovemaking, reaching out to a necessary conclusion. But it continues to elude us, staying just beyond our reach.

Exhausted, covered in sweat, my throat parched, my fingers numb, I remain a dead weight on her, my face in the fragrance of her hair.

You are my wife, I think. You are my wife. But who are you? Who am I?

I must have fallen asleep like that, and only become aware again of where I am when she moves under me and pushes me aside.

'You're too heavy,' she whispers.

'I'm sorry.'

'Don't be.' Her fingers are moving through my hair.

'I don't know what happened,' I say numbly. 'Something just didn't—'

'Don't talk now,' she says. 'It was good. There needn't always be an earthquake. You know that.'

'We just need a little time to get used to each other,' I assure her, without thinking.

Sarah makes an abrupt movement to raise her upper body and look at me. 'What on earth do you mean?' she asks. 'We've been married for nine years, for heaven's sake.'

There is a sinking feeling in my gut, but I make an effort: 'In a way every time is the first time,' I say. 'Don't you agree?'

She stares hard at me for a while, then slowly settles back into her previous position. For a while neither says anything.

Then, suddenly, she moves her head against mine. 'It was good,' she repeats in my ear. 'Wasn't it?'

'Yes, it was. Of course it was.'

'Are you going to sleep now?' she asks.

'Yes. And you?'

'Yes.' And after a moment, 'Will you hold my hand?'

We lie awake for a long time. I can hear it in her breathing, feel it in the unyielding tension of her body, lithe and sticky with sweat against mine.

In the morning, I think, I shall return to her. And take my time. To inspect everything that makes her. Her eyes and mouth and ears, her hair. Her shoulders, her arms and hands, each finger separately. Her nipples. Down to her toes. Everything. Everything. I must know who she is. I must find out what it means to say; 'Sarah'.

nine

But I do not fall asleep. My thoughts remain preoccupied, thinking of what has happened and not happened. Of what may yet happen.

I know that much of what has gone wrong tonight – no, that is not it: nothing has gone wrong, it has merely not gone right – has not to do with us, here, in this bed, but comes from very far back. Memories which I thought – hoped – had long been laid to rest. Lydia, of course. But also Embeth. Perhaps Embeth above all.

It was pure coincidence (but what is coincidence?) that we met. Initially, I had not even been selected as one of the artists invited to participate in the *South Africa?* exhibition in the new gallery at the top of Hout Street that November, but then somebody dropped out and I became a last-minute replacement, not even featured in the catalogue. Two of my paintings were accepted. The first featured a young woman, the left half of her body naked, the other half clothed very formally; the second showed two women, one seen from the back, the other from the front, one white, the other coloured. The pose was not erotic; it was merely a study in contrasting colours (even if I had used the same woman as a model for both figures). My style, I suppose, had initially been strongly influenced by the Nabis and less obviously by German expressionists, Otto Mueller in particular, still one of my favourites, although by that time I think I had begun to find my own vernacular. Those two canvases actually marked a new beginning.

For me, the exhibition opening represented a significant milestone as it was the first time I was exhibiting with more-or-less professional artists. The swirling, milling, sweat-smelling, wine-swilling crowd on the rainy afternoon of the opening included a fair number of visitors lured from the street primarily by the free drinks.

It was a heady experience. I even sold one of my two paintings, the one of the two women, titled *Sisters*. For the umpteenth time I dared to think a thought which has been hovering in my mind for most of my adult life: that, perhaps, teaching need not be the only career choice open to me.

Somewhere in the course of the afternoon she came to me. The young woman with the smoky dark eyes and the long lashes and the provocative mouth, dressed in faded denims and a stark white long-sleeved shirt with most of the buttons undone. Her skin a smooth, even brown that became paler where the shirt was folded back. I had noticed her earlier in the crowd – it was impossible not to – but in close-up she was devastating.

'You done this?' she asked point-blank, with a swing of her head to indicate my painting.

'I'm afraid so.'

'Why "afraid"?'

'Just a way of putting it.'

'A very white way.'

'Why should it be a white way?'

She shrugged, as if it would be too boring to attempt an answer. After a moment she asked, 'They're not really sisters, are they?'

'I suppose there are many ways of being sisters.'

'They're not the same colour.'

'You have no white sisters?' I challenged her.

A sudden laugh, a full-blooded belly laugh, more generous than I would have expected. But once again she did not deign to answer. After a moment she asked, 'What are you trying to say?' She gestured towards the painting again. There was something intoxicating about her presence, the unabashed challenge in her attitude, the raw femininity of her closeness.

'It's a painting, not a lesson.'

'Cop-out.'

'I didn't mean it that way.'

'It came out that way.'

An unexpected smile – these quicksilvery changes of mood would become one of her most defining characteristics – and then she said, 'It is a fucking nice painting.' Her smoky eyes narrowed. 'One would almost think they're the same girl.'

'You're very perceptive. They're both the same model.'

'Hm.' For a moment she gazed intently at the canvas. 'So which one is real, which one fake?'

'They're both equally real.'

'But the model.' A touch of irritableness in her voice. 'Was she coloured, or white?'

'Does it really matter?'

'It does to me.'

I hesitated. 'If you must know, she was white.'

'Could have thought so.' Her voice a sneer.

'Why?'

'I don't think you could handle a coloured woman, mister.'

Suddenly, recklessly, I took the plunge: 'Will *you* model for me?'

Without a moment's hesitation she said, 'Of course not.'

'Now *you* are scared.'

'I'm not. I'm just not interested.'

'Pity.'

'Pity for you or for me?'

'Who knows. Perhaps for both of us.'

There was a pause. Then, with a small laugh she turned and began to walk away. I could not make out whether I had won the round, or dismally lost it. But after a moment she came back.

'Tell me,' she said in a voice which was low and gravelly, 'do you fuck your models?'

I met her gaze. 'Not as a rule,' I said. 'It has happened.' It took some effort not to look away. 'But I prefer not to get involved.'

'And if I posed for you?'

'Then I would probably not.'

'Because you're scared or because I'm coloured?'

'Because it would not be very professional.'

'You're too clever by half.'

'I'm just trying to be sensible.'

'Oh God. *Please!*'

For a moment everything seemed spoiled. Then I said, trying my best to keep up a pretence of composure, 'Well? Where can I get in touch with you?'

'Leave it to me,' she said, tapping with a fingernail on her catalogue. Her little smile was inscrutable. And she turned to go.

But I followed her, suddenly in a panic. She *could* not go now!

'At least tell me your name!' I blurted out.

She looked back over her shoulder. 'I'll let you know if I get in touch.'

And then she was gone. I am the one, I thought dully, obtusely, who had missed his chance.

Somebody put a proprietorial hand on my arm. 'And who was the miss?' asked Nelia.

ten

Now, lying next to Sarah, one hand resting very lightly on her smooth brown shoulder, I allow all the memories slowly to ripple over me again, and I revisit them as if they belong to an old movie I have not seen in a long time.

I remember Nelia's words, the studied casualness in her voice, but also the darker undertone of suspicion.

'Just a fan,' I hear myself replying to her question, turning it into playful teasing. 'You'll have to get used to having a famous artist for a fiancé. I have actually sold a painting.'

'You've sold paintings before,' she reminded me.

'But only to friends or friends-of-friends,' I said. 'Not at an exhibition. From tonight I am in a new league, my love.'

She looked after the figure disappearing in the crowd.

'I don't think my parents will like the idea,' she said, clouds covering her frank blue eyes. 'Nor will yours.'

'Jesus, Nelia!' I exploded. 'I've just met the woman. It's not as if I'm going to jump into bed with her.'

She just stared at me, hurt and incomprehension in her face. And indeed, now that I think back, that was a turning point. *The* turning point, for her, for me, placing suddenly at risk everything we had previously taken for granted, everything that had been so predictable and safe.

We had practically grown up together, Nelia and I. My father enjoyed reminding us, especially when we had guests, of how we had been potty-trained together, sitting on our small plastic pots, one blue, one pink, on two corners of the newly bought yellow carpet in the lounge, diagonally across, our little faces red with the effort of trying to produce something to justify the family pride. Our parents had been at the University of Pretoria together; our fathers had regularly compared notes about their weekly progress with their respective girlfriends; they had married within months of each other. And on the very day of the yellow carpet they had jocularly agreed that one day the two of us would also be joined in wedlock to seal the friendship. They had so much in common – even though Nelia's father, a doctor, was in the eyes of the two mothers a small notch above mine on the social scale, mine being a mere teacher like me (though he later became a principal, then inspector of schools). In politics, in the church council, in municipal affairs, even in the tennis club, our fathers were peers, and fiercely benevolent competitors – as were our mothers in the Women's Auxiliary, in the charity drives sponsored by the church, and in cooking, baking, sewing, knitting or arranging flowers.

And then it was all fucked up by Embeth's appearance on the scene.

For ten days after the opening of the exhibition there was no sign of her. By that time, in spite of going to the gallery at least twice every day, I had given up on ever hearing from her again. (On the third day, coinciding with an unexpectedly glowing mention in a *Cape Times* review, the second painting was sold, and in the evening the two families celebrated together – even though they had been rather tight-lipped all the way about my penchant for nudes.) Then she telephoned. I would have recognised that voice anywhere, but it was so unexpected that I couldn't believe it; and the name, of course, meant nothing to me.

'Is that David le Roux?'

'Yes, I am. And you are . . .?'

'Embeth Arendse.'

'Embeth?' I asked. 'I'm afraid I don't—'

'Don't tell me you're *still* afraid?'

'You mean . . .?'

'You asked me to pose for you, remember? Or are there so many women crowding you that you cannot keep track of them all?'

'So that's your name?' I asked inanely.

'My parents called me Emma Elizabeth, but when I was three I changed it to Embeth and refused to listen if anybody tried to call me something else.'

'Precocious child.'

'You still interested in a model?'

'Not just any model. You.' A brief pause.

'And you promise not to fuck me?'

'All I promised was that I would try to behave properly.'

'Which may mean anything, of course.'

'Exactly.'

After a moment she said, 'I saw you've sold your other painting too. So you can't be too bad.'

That meant that she had actually gone back to the gallery. But I thought it prudent not to mention it.

'When can you come?' I asked, trying to keep my voice neutral.

'Sometime over the weekend?'

For a moment it was difficult to control my breathing. Then I said, 'Why not?' and she hung up.

She came on the Sunday afternoon, a sweltering day. My apartment, in a rundown building in a nondescript little street in Gardens, was like a baking oven, even though I'd had the fan running since early morning.

'Jesus!' she exclaimed as I opened the door for her. 'You do make sure that no one can keep their clothes on, don't you?' And she had barely crossed the threshold before she stepped out of the few bits of clothing she was wearing: a deep pink sleeveless top, white shorts, tiny orange knickers, thong sandals.

As a painter I was obviously not unfamiliar with the unclothed female body, but this took me by surprise. Not only because it happened so quickly, so casually, so matter-of-factly, but because Embeth was exquisitely beautiful. Small and frail without her clothes, like a pixie, with short-cropped hair and singularly graceful hands and feet.

Lying behind Sarah, her tight buttocks cupped by my lower belly and my thighs, my hands now pensively moulding her shoulders, then her breasts, I keep my eyes closed to reimagine Embeth. Two bodies so very different – one delicate and bird-like, the other long and lithe – and yet inexplicably, liquidly, merging with one another, like the shapes of dreams in sleep.

On that first Sunday Embeth posed for just over three hours before I wrapped it up. I had made twelve or fifteen sketches, and drawn rough outlines for two paintings on canvas.

'Well?' she asked as I closed the sketch pad and put away the charcoal pencils. 'Satisfied?'

'You were bloody good,' I said. Now that the session was over, I found it difficult to look at her. 'Shall I get us something to drink?'

It seemed as if she was going to say something, then thought better of it. When I returned from the kitchen, she had put on her skimpy bits of clothing; but she was still barefoot, dangling a string sandal from one big toe where she sat in a wicker chair much too big for her.

Over the next few months I saw a lot of her, but I cannot say I came to know her better. She kept her life to herself and simply saw no need to share any of her secrets with me. I did not even know where she lived. And yet I think, now, that this was exactly why I became so attracted to her. For the first time in my tidily defined life the future was not predictable. She was a wholly unknown factor. In her lurked, who knows, danger of a kind I could not explain. And I felt possessive about her strangeness. Here, at last, was somebody, something, exclusively – and exquisitely – *mine*.

There was something wild even in the rashness of the first moment I blurted out, 'Embeth, I love you!'

Her answer was shockingly matter-of-fact:

'Then fuck me.'

And so we did.

I still remember it with painful precision, here where I lie with my hands on the breasts of a strange woman who believes I am her husband, because that was the day our lives changed. In the most melo-dramatic way imaginable. Nelia walking in on us. Her face as she stood in the doorway, staring down at the two of us on the floor. No longer joined at the hip, but still naked.

Her funny little falsetto whisper: 'David . . .?'

And Embeth getting up – not scrambling, not furtively, but calmly, almost proudly – to collect her scattered clothes, and taking her time getting dressed. After what seemed to have been an unconscionable time, still without saying a word, she went to the front door with its frosted-glass panels, carrying her shiny red sandals in her right hand. (That is the one image I shall remember forever from that day: the red sandals.) Nelia's high-pitched voice: 'With a *meid*, David? David, with a *meid*?'

The very day after the end of our world, Embeth was priceless when she mimicked Nelia: 'With a *meid*, David? David, with a *meid*?'

But we were in a dead end. By time that Nelia had

already told her parents, and her parents had told my parents, and there was a grotesque gathering of all concerned.

I pleaded with Embeth: why should we allow our lives to be dictated by the unreasonable reasonableness of my family? If we loved each other . . .

'So what do you think we'll do?' she asked, a harsh tone of accusation in her voice. 'Pretend it's okay and nothing has happened?'

'We can go on as before,' I insisted.

'Will you run away with me?'

'Where to?'

'Overseas. London. Anywhere. As long as we get out of this place.'

'There's no call for anything drastic, Embeth.'

'And suppose I'm pregnant?'

'Are you?'

'It was only yesterday you took me, David!'

'What are you trying to say?'

'You want children with me? You want to go and show them to Oupa and Ouma?'

'Embeth, please! We can sit down and discuss this like grown-ups.'

'Like hell we can.' And again she mocked in that high-pitched voice, 'With a *meid*, David? David, with a *meid*?'

'She was hysterical. They were all unreasonable.'

'You're scared. I told you that very first day: you're scared.'

'Of what?'

'Of taking a decision. Of choosing, for once, what you want to do, not your fucking family.'

'Why should we be in such a hurry? We can take our time.'

'I can't see the point of letting this drag on and on.'

'Let's first see what happens.'

'No. You make up your mind. Like *now*.'

'It's not fair.'

'Then just fuck off.'

And so she left. This time she was wearing the red sandals, not carrying them in her hand.

85

Through the intervening years I have put the whole memory of Embeth safely and securely out of reach. But tonight it is suddenly back, flooding my conscience and my consciousness. As if, with me, it has slipped in through the blue door that once seemed so familiar.

eleven

In the early dawn, when the first light comes filtering into the bedroom, I start caressing Sarah whose body is still half folded into mine. I lie against her like a shipwreck against a curving dune, tracing her undulating outline with my hand. The rounded sweep of her hip, moving over her ribcage to trace the arc of a breast, feeling the nipple stir and stiffen under my touch. I am aching with desire. Most of the night I have floated on or just below the surface of sleep, not wanting to awaken her, but hardly able to contain my urgency, to resume from where we left off last night.

Even before my eyes can scan her face to see again what I have seen before, only more intensely now, more assuredly, more possessively, I recall the images of the first time, the very dark eyes half-closed, a thin snail-trail of saliva running from the corner of her ample mouth, a small frown of concentration between her eyebrows.

Half awake, she stirs, first moves as if to turn away, then shifts to her back to make herself more accessible, one leg drawn up. A small sigh. The hint of a welcoming smile.

'David . . . ?' she mumbles.

'I'm here,' I whisper. 'I'm all here.'

My hand moves across the crinkly roughness of her mound, two fingers probe the entrance to her sex, feeling for the minuscule slick puckering of her clitoris. With one hand she pushes the sheet down to her thighs.

And then there is a low thundering of feet and two ululating whoops of joy as the children come charging through the door and hurl themselves onto the bed, landing right between us. Instinctively we both roll away to make room for them, as we frantically try to cover ourselves. They do not even seem to notice our nakedness as they wriggle and writhe and roll over us and choke us with wild demonstrations of love and small wet mouths cover our faces with saliva and snot. Tommie, especially, is wheezing and snorting most alarmingly.

'You got a cold, lovey?' asks Sarah as she gathers him in her arms and presses him against her. His nose leaves an oystery smudge on her cheek.

Tommie nods fiercely, then breaks into a wide grin. 'But you know what? The wind got a cold too, I heard him sniffing outside all night.'

'Tonight we'll put out a *big* handkerchief for him, then he can blow his nose. Okay?'

'And a blanket,' proposes Tommie, 'so he won't get so cold again.'

'The wind doesn't need a blanket, silly,' Emily sneers with a puckered nose. 'He's got the clouds.'

'When I was a grown-up,' says Tommie, 'I also slept under the clouds.'

'We don't want to be late for school,' says Sarah, swinging her legs out of the bed. My eyes dwell on the curve of her back. 'Come on. Daddy can help Emily, I'll dress you.'

'I can dress myself,' Tommie says. 'I'm big enough.'

'You can't even tie your shoelaces,' Emily jeers.

'I can too.'

'You can't.'

'I can!'

'Let's see who gets done first.' In a flash the little fairy-girl is out of her tiny nightie and running down the passage.

The next hour is a whirlwind of comings and goings, running and jumping, teasing and taunting, laughter and tears, chasing and fleeing, hiding and seeking, all of it with a total commitment to every new moment, an energy that leaves me breathless. At last everybody is clean and fed, and Sarah prepares to drive them to crèche and preschool.

'You want me to come with?' I ask at the kitchen

door, thinking it might be an easy introduction to the morning routine, and the route to school, in case I have to take over some time.

But Sarah shakes her head. Imprinting a brief kiss on my cheek she says, already on her way to the small red Corsa parked under a lean-to behind the kitchen: 'I'm going to have tea with Brenda afterwards. And I know you have more than enough to do before the exhibition.'

What exhibition, I wonder?

From the kitchen door I wave and spontaneously call, 'Bye. Love you.'

Unexpectedly, she stops to turn.

'I love you, David!' she calls back. Then she unlocks the car door for the children and they storm in, scrambling and whooping.

To my own surprise, I ask, 'Why do you love me?'

Sarah comes the few steps back to me. She reaches out and puts her hands on my shoulders. With unexpected seriousness she says, very softly, 'Because you make me possible.'

And then she goes back to the car. I watch them as they drive off.

Please come back! I want to plead. But I do not speak the words.

An almost eerie silence descends on the house.

Where shall I begin? There is a whole world waiting to be discovered, probed, registered for future reference. And now that I am alone, the place feels precarious, menaced from all sides. Will it not suddenly cave in under me? Will all kinds of new doors swing open before me, leading to God knows what unpredictable spaces, what new threatening or welcoming strangers?

As a precaution I return to the front door where it all started yesterday. Hesitate with my hand on the doorknob, then turn it. I am conscious of a tightness in my chest. The door swings open. The outside is the same deep blue I first painted it, and looks exactly as it has looked for years. The bit of flaking paint, the two parallel scratches near the keyhole. I remember the feeling of exultation with which I painted it. My declaration of independence. My door. My space. Mine, mine only. In which I could do whatever I wished without anybody else – not even my own wife – knowing where I was or what I was up to. I remember how I first set upon the surface (a dreary, ordinary brown, a kind of civil-service brown, at the time), covering it with wild and uncontrolled strokes in all directions. How I imagined strange faces, shapes, animals, humans looming up from the mysterious ultramarine depths, appearing and disappearing, changing, transmuting. All of it mine. That was before Lydia followed me here and colonised my space.

Back inside. Closing the door meticulously behind me. First to the master bedroom. It is all still there. The clothes strewn on the floor, the cupboard door ajar, the bed crumpled. I kneel beside it, push away the blankets and press my face into the sheets. They bear a faint odour of bodies, of sex, us. Unless I am imagining it all; unless I have imagined it.

I tarry there – scared, perhaps, of what I may find in the rest of the house? This room, at least, is a space

I know by now. I close my eyes to call up again the image of the strange, beautiful, young woman who thinks of me as her husband and who believes that I am the father of her children. Anxious to savour the moment, I stay on to make the bed. Then turn to face the built-in cupboards and work systematically through all the shelves and hanging space. One whole section is taken up by men's clothes, presumably mine. On the whole I approve of the taste they reveal, although there are a few rather disreputable old jeans and shirts among them. Rummaging through them I discover a shirt I recognise. It gives me a strange sense of belonging, even though I don't have the faintest idea of how it ever got here. Then a few more shirts. Two pairs of trousers. Some underpants that can do with mending or throwing away. They must indeed be mine. I shrug, hesitating between relief and alarm.

After that I inspect the women's clothes, mostly with approval. Excellent taste, particularly in casual dresses and underwear, erring on the side of youth: minidresses, sexy sandals, thongs and G-strings. In one drawer, a large collection of jewellery, flashing and funky and fun. I like this person. I could live with her. I do live with her.

From the bedroom I proceed to the en suite bathroom, still in delightful disarray presumably from Sarah's ablutions last night before I used it and came to bed.

But then I become impatient. The rest of the house is waiting. God knows what lurks behind each new door.

There are pictures in the passage. A couple of my paintings: I do not recognise them individually, but the style is familiar. It has taken me a long time to arrive at this point. In the beginning my work was eclectic, perhaps even haphazard. At one stage I moved into abstraction. Fun, but immensely frustrating in the long run: I felt threatened and oppressed by the limitless freedom it implied, the tyranny of freedom. What I needed was discipline, some kind of framework – if only to challenge it with the possibilities of breaking out of it. That was when the Nabis began to point the way. At least it made me feel safe. Though I always remained conscious of an urge to break free more radically, to take risks, to place my certainties at stake, I could never quite abandon the need for the reassurance of the familiar.

There are other pictures in the passage too. A few, unmistakably, done by the children. Also a couple of large framed photographs. Black and white. One portrait of a woman: her head draped in a dark cloth that hangs loosely over one shoulder, leaving the other exposed; and with a nipple visible in the bottom left corner. An intriguing face, largely in shadow. It takes a while before I recognise her. It is Sarah. My immediate reaction is jealousy, suspicion: who was the photographer? But there is no clue to his identity at all, except that I sense it must have been a man. Only a man could have insisted so darkly on the eroticism of that nipple.

The second bedroom is the children's. No dark surprises here. Once again I linger to make the two small beds and tidy up the mess.

There is a third bedroom. On the wall, another of my paintings, and two photographs, starkly stylised, and once again in black and white. No signature, no clues; but for some reason I have no doubt that they must be the work of the same photographer. For a moment I catch myself wondering whether it could be Sarah's husband – until it strikes me that *I* am her husband. Supposed to be.

Lounge. Dining room. Kitchen. The second bathroom, where I bathed the children last night. Another, shorter, passage branches off from the main one. What immediately strikes me is the series of photographs on the wall, ten or twelve of them, quite close together, all in black and white, all of doors, some ajar, most of them closed. Wonderfully textured shots, printed in heavy grain, all divorced from the buildings to which they must have belonged. Just doors, doors. And the cumulative effect is over-whelming. A sense of secrecy, of secretness, doors not only to the unknown but the unknowable, their mysteries forever out of reach. I cannot make out whether they are ominous, louring, threatening – or simply blank, unsettling in their very ordinariness. They force me to look round to where I have just come from, expecting perhaps to see some stranger on my heels, man or alien, or even the woman of the house herself, the one who goes by the name of Sarah and who first opened the blue door to me to invite me into her secret space. Which turned out to be merely a house. Her house. Presumed to be mine. The house where I live. Where I may have been living for years.

After the series of photographs there are two more doors in the side passage, one open, one closed. A door in natural dark wood – not plywood but solid, impressively solid, forbiddingly solid. Should I risk it? But how can I not?

For a long time I remain standing in front of the closed door. A very, very ordinary door. So ordinary that it makes my skin turn to gooseflesh.

I don't want to go in here. What are those famous words that still make men cringe after six hundred years? – *Abandon all hope, ye who enter.*

Bloody ridiculous.

This is *my* house. It should have no secrets for me.

I push it open.

The door opens to a very untidy room. Quite big, probably six metres by seven or thereabouts. It is a studio. A photographic studio. Two large-format cameras on tripods. Several others, 35 mm, strewn across two trestle tables, almost as if a very hectic session has been interrupted midway. Against the far wall, a wide roll of black paper, some three metres across, hanging from a beam. Various items of furniture: easy chairs, a swing suspended from the ceiling. Bits and pieces of clothing draped everywhere: scarves and shawls, dresses, tops, stockings, knickers, bras.

There are photographs on all the walls. These are not framed, but pinned haphazardly to large softboards. On both the tables are stacks of other photographs, some threatening to topple over.

After wandering about in some bewilderment I decide to start from the door and work my way anticlockwise around the studio.

The photos are of an astounding variety, city-scapes, trees, groups of people, cats, individual faces. Yet it does not take long to acknowledge that they must all be by the same photographer. The majority are studies of women, their faces and bodies obscured, but also dramatically moulded, by shadow. Still intrigued by the anonymity of the photographer, I start hunting for clues.

I am halfway round the room before the answer becomes obvious. There is a whole collection of intimate shots, a number of them nude, others with underwear in the process of being put on, or taken off; some of which show only parts of the body: an elbow, a shoulder, a torso in three-quarters profile, a ribcage, a breast, a stomach with the indentation of the navel staring like a vacant eye. All of them obviously taken in a mirror, which is incorporated in the composition. Sometimes two mirrors, or even three, in such as way that an endless dialogue between reflections is triggered. The series concludes with several shots of the photographer in close-up, distorted by the mirrors, either with a fragment of the body visible, slightly out of focus, below the face, or showing the face only, the single-reflex lens like a huge Cyclops eye peering at the spectator. It is not a man after all. It is, every time, Sarah. No doubt at all.

After facing this disturbing series I cannot absorb much more; and the rest of my tour is more cursory. I can, after all, always come back.

Moving down the passage to the last door in the side passage, I start feeling less agitated. Already I have a presentiment of where this will lead to. And my hunch turns out to be right: all the signs point to it being my own studio. The studio which, as I remember it, used to take up most of my rented cottage with the blue door.

But it is still not without surprises: quite a number of the paintings are ones I am sure I have taken home long ago. A few, I remember very clearly, have been sold. What is most unnerving is that two of them are the paintings which were shown at the very first group exhibition where I met Embeth. The one of the girl split in two, one half immaculate and formally dressed, the other half naked; the second of the white and coloured girls, one approaching, the other going.

I close my eyes for a moment. I must not lose my head now.

Finding it unbearable to face that pivotal moment from my past any longer, I return to the main passage and head for the kitchen. Time for a cup of tea, a few minutes of rest to gather my thoughts and plan my day. But there is a sense of inconclusiveness about the morning. Something continues to bother me.

From the kitchen I go back along the side passage to the first of the two studio doors. Impossible to avoid them, most particularly the first one, behind the closed door. I must see more of Sarah. I must come closer to solving the riddle she poses in her work – as a pointer, perhaps, to the riddle of herself.

The first thing that strikes me as I open the door to her studio again is that the sequence and configuration of the photographs on the walls appear to have changed. Several I do recognise, but now they are in different positions – that is, if I remember correctly; if my memory is to be trusted. But I realise that I may indeed be mistaken: except for that one series of self-portraits and nudes I may simply not have paid enough attention on my first visit. Suppressing the anxiety that I can feel building up inside me I start going round the walls again. This time my first – and worst – suspicions are confirmed: although I do not expect to recall every detail precisely, surely it is unlikely that so many of the photographs should appear altogether new this time round? The uneasiness persists.

It grows worse when I become aware of the fact that with *every* new round I make along the walls I seem to notice different things – not only in the configuration of the pictures, but in the images themselves. I remember specifically studying the portrait of a woman with a mantilla covering half her face, with a beauty spot prominent on the exposed cheek. It is mounted next to a rather shocking study of a girl doing a cartwheel. But on my next round they have shifted: the woman with the mole on her cheek has moved further along; the cartwheeling girl is no longer there.

I can feel a coldness quivering its way down my spine. I do not want to be here any longer.

But I must make one final round, to be absolutely certain. I advance one slow step at a time, trying to memorise as much as possible of each individual photo.

This time there is no doubt at all. The discovery comes when I reach, once again, the spot where I first saw the girl doing the cartwheel. She is still missing. But in her place there is a portrait of a face I know only too well.

Embeth.

How can I ever forget the contours of that face, those sad and ominous eyes, the mouth half open, the way I saw her in close-up in the throes of making love?

I have to go. Impossible to linger here a minute longer.

As I approach the door, my hand already outstretched to grasp the knob so that I can close it the moment I go out, another photograph, immediately to the left of the doorway, brings me to a standstill.

Lydia.

Her eyes – even in black and white I recognise their luminosity – gaze straight at me in what looks like accusation. And I can hear her voice as she said yesterday when I prepared to leave for the studio: 'Please don't forget to get the things at the supermarket. Remember they close earlier on Sundays. Have you got the list?'

'In my jeans pocket,' I said.

And then I left. And went to the supermarket after I'd finished my day's work. And returned to find myself here, at the blue door of this house. And when, later, I tried to go back to our apartment building, there was no way in.

I am terrified to stay in this room surrounded by these photographs, yet I cannot move, I'm unable to tear myself away. I cannot leave before glancing around the room one last time.

Faces, faces, unmasked, stripped bare, stare at me. The others – the cityscapes, the figures, the group studies, the cats – have all disappeared. Only the portraits remain. The staring faces with their eyes, their mouths, their foreheads, their eyes, their eyes. I know them all. In one way or another they have all played a part in my life.

I must go. First of all, I must find Lydia again. I cannot stay here. I have never felt so exposed, so threatened, in my life.

twelve

There is something inevitable about this trip, back to Lydia. The city surrounding me has an air of detachment, of remoteness, as if it is waiting for whatever is to happen, without intending to interfere or get involved in any way. I drive along Eastern Boulevard, with the sea and the harbour below on my left. In the middle distance, a brownish smudge in the cerulean, cobalt blue and turquoise and ultramarine of the ocean, lies Robben Island. Now almost irrelevant, canonised by history, no longer a defining presence, unless one chooses to remember. What is past is past. Or is it? Is returning to Lydia not in its own way an attempt to retrieve the past?

Lydia. But, behind her, Embeth too. The day she left with her red sandals in her hand. The day she kept them on. The utter finality of that goodbye. Even in dreams she was cancelled, enclosed behind a door no one and nothing could open again.

Yet it was not a complete return to the bosom of my family either: we would never feel quite comfortable with one another again. They forgave me for my 'aberration' - but the very fact that they believed I needed forgiveness, drew an invisible screen between us.

It took a long time to adapt to the new phase of my life. But the curious thing about knowing that Embeth could not form part of it, was also a kind of release. Something deep inside me had closed for good. For good or bad. Something would remain forever unfulfilled, unrealised, unthinkable. But I was also free. To move on. To whatever lay ahead.

And perhaps - no, not perhaps, but undoubtedly - that was one of the reasons why I was ready to meet

Lydia when she made her appearance in my life a few years after Embeth disappeared from it.

I remember going to the shop selling artists' materials in a somewhat seedy side street off Lansdowne Road. I needed a few camel-hair brushes and some tubes of paint – cobalt blue, vermilion, cadmium yellow. I'd known the manager and his wife, the Laubschers, for years, ever since they'd moved from the old shop in Long Street; but this morning was the first time I'd met their daughter Lydia, who had then just finished her degree in architecture at UCT and was helping them out during the holidays. A rather stormy meeting in the happy confusion of the little shop which had always been a tranquil little refuge in the past (and known for the fine, freshly ground coffee they served to old customers). This time there was a lot of shouting going on, an altercation between a very big customer with an untidy mop of hair and large stained hands, and Lydia, whom I'd never seen before, petite and delicate behind the counter, her red hair flaming in a shaft of morning sunshine that slanted through the side window.

'Don't you tell me about what green to use!' the customer was shouting. 'I wanted sap green, not this stupid cobalt green.'

'Why didn't you check the tube before you left? And anyway, you said you were painting a eucalyptus tree, and sap green is too bright for that.'

'You turned my painting into a bloody mess and I had to come all the way back. Is that the way to treat an artist?'

'Nobody who uses this colour for eucalyptus trees is an artist's backside,' sneered the young woman. 'You should paint walls, not canvases.' Her eyes, I noticed immediately, were themselves a most intense cobalt green, with touches of amber.

'That's what comes from putting a woman behind the counter in an artists' shop!' stormed the burly man. 'I demand a new tube of green.'

'And I won't exchange it because you've already used up half the tube.'

'One little squeeze, that's all I used,' he raged.

'This is not one squeeze. Look!' She grabbed the tube from him, unscrewed it in a single deft flick of her wrist and pressed.

Neither of them could have expected what followed: a long, slimy green worm of paint came flying from the tube and hit the customer in the face.

'You clumsy clot!' he roared, reaching for her across the counter.

I am not a big man, certainly not compared to that bellowing beast; and I usually avoid anything remotely resembling public brawls or tussles. But this was an emergency, and the two of them were so grossly mismatched that I had no choice. I grabbed the big man's arm from behind and pulled him away from the counter. He was off balance already and the unexpected jerk caused him to stagger back to the door. At that moment another customer came in, accompanied by the girl's father. The situation was defused. The new customer moved in between the counter and the aggressor; in spite of the young woman's protests, her father offered a tube of paint (sap green) to the bearded, gesticulating man, who decided to leave, still dabbing at his smudged face with a dirty handkerchief and muttering imprecations under his breath.

It took a few cups of very strong coffee for the tempers to settle down, but soon both Mr Laubscher and his daughter could laugh about the outburst. Both of them had a delightful sense of fun, of humour, of generosity. And in due course Lydia and I discovered more and more reasons to spend time together. She was very busy at that stage of her life, involved as she was with several community projects in which her skills as an architect and her strong sense of civic responsibility stood her in good stead, so we did not always have much time to ourselves. But I was attracted by her warmth, her spontaneity, her passion about 'doing something' after the drastic changes that had occurred in the country.

We were married just over a year after the day in the shop. For her it meant finding a firm foundation for doing what she really wanted to do. For me, it was a return to normality – no, not normality, but the mere *possibility* of a normality interrupted by Embeth.

As it turned out, for neither of us was there happiness ever after. Only on rare – and relatively unimportant – occasions did I see further signs of her delightful, unreasonable temper, her uncontrolled passion; marriage seemed to bridle her and restrain her, curbing her natural exuberance in anticipation of motherhood. Whereas I . . . ? I settled into the predictabilities of matrimony. The old dream of giving up teaching and painting full-time was continually postponed – no longer because it was regarded, as Nelia and her parents had done, as unworthy and romantic, but because I myself felt the need to be a provider, not an escapist. On the other hand, I would never again feel free either. I had made a move, but not far enough. I had never arrived 'on the other side' of whatever it might have been. An in-betweenness would be the most I could hope for. But it was better than nothing. Wasn't it?

Lydia's dedication to the projects she was involved with – a school in Crossroads, a crèche in Khayelitsha, a vast housing scheme in Delft, a recreation centre in Lavender Hill – made it difficult to lead a relaxed life together; but the fulfilment she derived from her work made it worthwhile. And I was happy to support her while I kept the back door to my own ambition open. Of course, what was really missing from the marriage was children. Both our sets of parents were pressing for grandchildren; for various reasons – many of which we could not even bring ourselves to discuss – we, too, wanted a family. But it did not work out like that. Not for lack of trying! It just never happened. At one stage I suggested that we go for tests, but Lydia – strangely – refused. It didn't 'feel right' to her. We learned to adapt; but there was the emptiness of an ache between us, and in time it grew more, not less, urgent. I could see the difference it gradually made to Lydia, how her green eyes began to lose their spark; and we both started filling the gap with other activities, with social obligations, with money. I learned to paint what the market wanted. Lydia accepted contracts that had less and less to do with the community, more with increasing her visibility.

I don't think it really bothered us all that much. And perhaps that was the worst part of it? A 'good life', a 'working marriage'. Security.

Until, suddenly, yesterday, if it was only yesterday, a blue door closed between us. And now I know just how important it has become for us to talk. To talk properly about it all.

I remember how she once told me about her love of swings when she was small. How she always wanted to go higher and higher, and then suddenly to shout at her father to run and catch her, and then to let go, wildly, madly, irresponsibly, absolutely confident that he would arrive in the nick of time to pluck her from the air and press her against him; and the smell of green grass when they fell down together and laughed, and knew that the world was a good place to be in. And how, in later years, she started having nightmares about it, with her father arriving too late, or not at all.

And feeling how that early faith and trust began to be eroded, and filtered away. From then on there was the need, ever more urgent, to find other forms of security. In her work, in me, in friends. She became almost paranoid in her fear of the unpredictable. The very wildness, the freedom, the ecstasies of her early years slowly turned into a terror of the things that had made life worth living before.

I don't know why all of this should be coming back to me now, on this radiant early summer morning. But I do know that I have to get back to her, to have and to hold her again, tightly, securely. I must return to that huge building that so unexpectedly let me down last night. I still have no explanation for what happened. It can only have been some kind of delusion. But today, in this unequivocal sunshine, I know it will be different. She will be there. She must be. And this bizarre dream I have been imagining since yesterday, since the moment I stepped through that blue door, will be over.

(But where will Sarah be then? Sarah with the graceful curve of her brown hip, the empty eye of her navel in her pale belly, the round perfection of her breasts, the deep gravelly sound of her voice? And the two lovely children, our children, Emily and little Tommie? And the photographs? All those unsettling faces, those shadows and brush strokes of light?)

I turn off from Edinburgh Drive, move into the smaller streets, head for the gigantic building I know so well and which changed the aspect of the whole suburb when it was built.

But it is not there.

I could not possibly have been mistaken!

I find parking on a yellow line and set out on foot. Double-check the street names, even though I know them by heart. Everything exactly as – and how – it is supposed to be. But the building is missing. As if the suburb has reverted to what it used to be, long ago, before planners and builders and developers and architects (Lydia among them) moved in. Claremont Towers is no longer there. Not there at all.

After half an hour of increasingly desperate searching, I approach a group of bergies on a sidewalk. Some are drinking from bottles wrapped in newsprint; one or two have passed out.

'Excuse me,' I say hesitantly. 'I'm looking for a block of flats. It's called Claremont Towers. Could any of you guys tell me how to get there?'

For a moment they interrupt their drinking to stare at me, then start conferring heatedly among themselves. But the verdict is negative.

'Never seen a place like that,' a spokesman informs me.

'Are you quite sure?' I demand.

'We been coming here to this place for years, sir. Mandela was still in jail, like, when we first come here. You sure it's not in Newlands or someplace?'

'I am absolutely sure.'

After a brief, embarrassed hesitation, I say, 'I live there.'

They go into a huddle again.

'Sorry, Master' – for greater emphasis the

spokesman has reverted to an obsolete form of address – 'but Master must be a little bit mistaken. No such place in these parts.'

Before it becomes more humiliating, I move off. Stop at one or two houses where gardeners in blue overalls or ladies in broad-brimmed straw hats are pottering in flower beds, and repeat my enquiries. No luck.

With ferocious determination I stride towards the shopping streets of the area. Printing shops, florists, household stores, antique dealers. Then right into the heart of the suburb. Cavendish Square.

Not a single person has any knowledge of the building. And yet I live there! (Don't I?) I was there last night. True, I couldn't find my way into the building, but *it was there*. For God's sake!

Back to my car. A pink ticket fluttering from the driver's window. I tear it off without looking, crumple it into a ball, chuck it away.

My building no longer exists. My apartment, number 1313 on the thirteenth floor, has disappeared like a boat in a fog. Lydia is no longer there.

There is nowhere else to turn to, nowhere at all. Except back to Green Point, where I have just come from.

Back to the blue door which I painted myself.

thirteen

Back along the Boulevard, up Strand Street into High Level Road, then a little way down and right, to where I used to park when I went to work in my studio. Now the place that has become my home. There is a feeling of resignation, perhaps even desolation in me. This is it. Will have to be it. But there is a touch of inexplicable joy too. At last to have something definite to come back to. As if, after years of dithering, of living a suspended existence, I have taken something resembling a firm decision. Now I *want* to be where I am.

I feel suddenly weary, the weariness that the little men in the children's story must have felt upon returning to their long, thin, white house after the dolphin had brought them back from the other side of the sea.

In my dream, it occurs to me, I lost wife and children. Here, today, I have found a new family. It makes sense after all.

I get out of the car and lock it. Open the side gate of the property and walk through it. Down, and then around to the front. Where, for once, I know exactly what will be waiting behind the blue door.

Except that this time the door was not blue. It was, I noticed as I took out my key to insert it into the lock, a deep and uncompromising cadmium yellow.

I pushed it in, took a deep, sad breath, turned the key, and pressed against the door.